Praise for The Imagination Station

[Imagination Station] books are full of adventure, [and teach about] God.

—Jesse, age 10, Midlothian, Texas

So far in our home-schooling journey with boys, The
Imagination Station series has, by far, been the books
that my boys have wanted to read the most. It's very
exciting to have content that I can trust!

—Chrystal H., home-school mom, Midlothian, Texas

The Redcoats Are Coming! will leave [students] riveted
to the journey and history in the story. A teacher will
be able to stop at any chapter and leave the children
waiting for more.

—Margaret G., teacher aide, Auburn, New York

The Redcoats Are Coming! will teach kids a lot of
valuable lessons about faith such as courage and hope.

—Irene R., children's author and editor, Ontario, Canada

More praise for The Imagination Station® books

I can't think of a better way for children to learn about United States history. This book is one not to be missed!

—Sharon B., public school teacher, Munster, Indiana

I love that the books are easy to read. I want to keep reading because the books are full of adventure!

—Kanaan, age 8, Midlothian, Texas

The Redcoats Are Coming! is a fun and exciting way for young readers to experience the history of our country while learning the importance that faith has played in many of the events. An excellent family-centered series that will engage readers of all ages.

—Terri F., children's author, Nashville, Indiana

A perfect history adventure for Christian School students and home-schoolers.

—Mona P., elementary volunteer reader, Appleton, Maine

FOCUS ON THE FAMILY PRESENTS

The Redcoats Are Coming!

BOOK 13

MARIANNE HERING • NANCY I. SANDERS
CREATIVE DIRECTION BY PAUL McCUSKER
ILLUSTRATED BY DAVID HOHN

TYNDALE

FOCUS ON THE FAMILY • ADVENTURES IN ODYSSEY®
TYNDALE HOUSE PUBLISHERS, INC. • CAROL STREAM, ILLINOIS

The Redcoats Are Coming!
© 2014 Focus on the Family

ISBN: 978-1-58997-774-7

A Focus on the Family book published by Tyndale House Publishers, Inc., Carol Stream, Illinois 60188.

Focus on the Family and Adventures in Odyssey, and the accompanying logos and designs, are federally registered trademarks, and The Imagination Station is a federally registered trademark of Focus on the Family, 8605 Explorer Drive, Colorado Springs, CO 80920.

TYNDALE and Tyndale's quill logo are registered trademarks of Tyndale House Publishers, Inc.

Cover design by Michael Heath | Magnus Creative

Library of Congress Cataloging-in-Publication Data
Hering, Marianne, author.
   The Redcoats are coming! / Marianne Hering, Nancy I. Sanders ; illustrated by David Hohn.
       pages cm. -- (Imagination Station; book 13)
Summary: On the eve of the American Revolution, Patrick and Beth travel back in time to deliver a letter to Paul Revere.
   ISBN 978-1-58997-774-7 (alk. paper)
   1. United States--History--Revolution, 1775-1783--Juvenile fiction. [1. United States--History--Revolution, 1775-1783--Fiction. 2. Time travel--Fiction. 3. Christian life--Fiction.] I. Sanders, Nancy I., author. II. Hohn, David, illustrator. III. Title.
   PZ7.H431258Rd 2014
   [Fic]--dc23
                                                2013046640
Printed in the United States of America
4 5 6 7 8 9 / 18 17 16

For manufacturing information regarding this product, please call 1-800-323-9400.

To Esther,

For your sweet, gentle smile, your talent in everything

creative, and your love of listening to Adventures in

Odyssey, just before you fall asleep at night . . .

this book is for you!

—NIS

Contents

Vacation Plans

Beth raced down the sidewalk toward Whit's End. Her footsteps pounded on the sidewalk. Patrick jogged behind her.

It was a hot summer day. Beads of sweat dripped down the back of Beth's neck.

All of a sudden Patrick raced past Beth. He reached the door to Whit's End first and pushed it open.

Beth was annoyed as she heard the bell on the door jingle. She wanted to be the first

to tell Whit the news.

She followed Patrick inside.

Whit stood at the cash register behind the counter. He handed some change to a customer. Then he pushed the drawer of the cash register closed.

Patrick stopped in front of the counter. He grabbed the edge with both hands.

"Guess what?" he said to Whit. "Grandma is taking us on a trip—"

"To Boston!" Beth said before

Patrick could finish. She saw a flash of irritation cross Patrick's face.

Beth moved to the counter next to her cousin.

Whit looked from Beth to Patrick. "Summer vacation plans?" he asked.

"Yes!" Beth said. The words tumbled out. "Grandma has been planning a surprise—"

"And my mom just told me today," Patrick said. "Grandma bought plane tickets—"

"And we get to leave tomorrow," Beth said. "So we have to pack right away."

Beth grinned at Patrick, and Patrick grinned back. Beth didn't feel annoyed anymore. Now she just felt excited.

"Why is Boston so special?" Whit asked.

"Boston is where the American Revolution started," Beth said. "We learned about it in school. Grandma wants us to see the places we learned about."

"That should make it all come alive," Whit said. "I have a Bible from the Revolutionary War. It's been in my family for generations."

"Cool!" Patrick said. "I'll bet it's worth a lot of money."

"Maybe," Whit said. "Though I'd never sell it."

"May we see it?" Beth asked.

"Of course," Whit said. Then he paused and rubbed his chin. "If I can remember where I put it."

"You don't know where it is?" Patrick asked. "How could you lose something as important as that?"

"I haven't lost it," Whit said. "I cleaned out my attic and moved a lot of things around. I think it's in a box . . ." Whit snapped his

4

fingers. "I remember where it is. Follow me!"

The cousins followed Whit down the stairs. The stairway led to his basement workshop.

They walked over to one of the workbenches. It was covered with screws and nails. Beth saw hammers and wrenches and what looked like electronic parts.

Whit reached under the workbench. He grabbed the handle of a wooden chest. It reminded Beth of a pirate's treasure chest.

"Umph!" said Whit. The wooden chest moved slightly. Whit pulled harder. The chest slid out from under the bench. "There."

He stood up and searched the top of the workbench. He smiled and grabbed a key. It was lying next to an old radio tube. He knelt down and put the key in the chest's lock. *Click.*

A Mysterious Letter

Whit opened the lid of the chest and reached inside. He lifted up a smaller, dusty box. He blew on the top of the box.

The cloud of dust made Beth sneeze.

"Sorry," Whit said as he lifted the lid of the smaller box. He carefully pulled out a large book. It had gold lettering on the spine. It was a Bible.

Beth saw how yellow and old the pages looked.

Whit set the Bible down on the table. He gently turned the pages.

Patrick gave a low whistle. "So they used this Bible during the American Revolution," he said. "It's over two hundred years old!"

Beth looked at the large book. "I guess it wasn't a pocket edition," she said.

Whit chuckled. "Only if they had extremely large pockets," he said. He turned to the Psalms.

An old yellow envelope slid out from the pages. It landed facedown on the table.

Beth saw a brown blob on the flap of the envelope. She thought the blob looked like a circle of melted crayon. It was cracked with age.

Whit looked puzzled. Then he picked up the envelope and turned it over. There was curly writing on the front of it. "I'd forgotten about this," Whit said.

"What is it?" asked Patrick.

Whit held up the envelope.

Beth gasped. The front of the envelope was addressed to Paul Revere.

Patrick's eyes went wide. "Paul Revere?" Patrick said. "Why do you have a letter to Paul Revere?"

"Who is it from?" Beth asked.

"It doesn't look opened," Patrick said. "Have you read it?"

Whit said, "Well—"

"What does it—" Patrick said.

"Don't interrupt him," Beth said.

"*You* did it too!" Patrick said.

"All right, you two," Whit said with a smile. "I know you're excited, but there's no need to argue."

"Please tell us the story of the letter," Beth said.

Patrick stepped closer. His eyes sparkled with anticipation.

Whit looked at the cousins. "I could tell you the story. But maybe you should experience it."

Beth clapped her hands. She knew what Whit was talking about. They were going on another adventure in the Imagination Station.

The machine was one of Whit's inventions. It was like a time machine. Whit used it to help history come to life.

The three of them turned to the
Imagination Station. It sat off to the side of
the room. The machine looked like the front
part of a helicopter. The doors stood open.

Whit handed the letter to Patrick. "You
can deliver the letter to Paul Revere
personally," Whit said.

Beth felt disappointed. *Why did Patrick
get to take the letter?* she wondered.

Whit nodded to Beth. He seemed to
understand what she was thinking. He
leaned over and dug around in the wooden
chest. He pulled out a white apron and
handed it to Beth.

"An apron?" she asked. The apron had
two strings at the top. The strings were for
tying around her waist. A white ruffle went
all around the apron's bottom edge. In the

front were two big pockets.

"Will I be cooking?" she asked.

"You'll see," Whit said.

Whit went to the side of the workbench. He drew a long stick from an old umbrella stand. He held it out to Patrick. "You better take this," he said.

"What's it for?" Patrick asked as he took the stick.

"It's a cane," Whit said. "*Always* keep it with you. You'll need it."

Beth watched as Patrick took the cane. He held it in his left hand. He still held Paul Revere's letter in the other.

Whit gestured toward the Imagination Station. The cousins climbed in and sat down on the cushy seats.

Whit moved to the control panel on the

side of the machine. He pushed several keys. The Imagination Station started to hum. Lights flashed on and off.

"Have a nice trip," Whit said. "And don't forget. Ask for ink if someone offers you a quill."

"What does that mean?" Beth asked.

But the doors to the Imagination Station slid closed. Whit didn't hear her.

Beth looked at Patrick. He shrugged and said, "I guess we'll find out."

Beth reached to push the red button.

The Imagination Station shuddered and shook. It rumbled. Then it rattled and whirred.

Beth felt strange. It was like being sucked into a giant vacuum. Then suddenly, everything went black.

3

Secret Code

Patrick shook his head. Then he opened his eyes.

The cousins were standing next to a fancy, large white building. It had four white columns standing on the front porch. Horse-drawn carriages were parked in front of it. Nearby, more horses were tied to posts.

A gust of wind blew past them. It picked up dust from the dirt road. Patrick also could smell the freshness of spring blossoms.

The Imagination Station slowly faded away and disappeared.

Patrick lifted his hand against the blowing dust. His eyes went to a steeple rising above the porch. A large bell hung in the steeple. The metal bell gleamed in the sun.

His hand brushed something on his head. It was a hat. He took it off. It was shaped like a triangle. "That's funny," he said.

"Look at your clothes," Beth said.

Patrick looked down. He wore a blue coat with a double row of shiny buttons. His tan pants looked like long shorts. They reached down just below his knees. Tall stockings and leather shoes with brass buckles completed his outfit. He tapped the side of his shoes with the cane.

"I feel like a proper gentleman," Patrick said.

Beth wore a long red dress that reached to the ground. It had white ruffles around the sleeves. A white collar was tied around her neck. She held her white apron in her hands.

"Should I put the apron on now?" she asked.

"I don't know," Patrick said. He held up the letter to Paul Revere. It looked brand new.

Suddenly, hoofbeats sounded behind them. Patrick turned around.

A girl rode up on a brown pony. The pony had a brown saddle. A saddlebag hung down on each side of the pony's back. Patrick thought they looked like big brown pockets.

The girl stopped her pony near Patrick and Beth. She gathered her long skirts in

her hand. Then she slid off the pony.

The new girl had long, blonde hair in a braid. She was about Beth's height. Her long tan dress and white apron looked homemade like Beth's.

But the girl's face looked older than Beth's. Patrick guessed she was a teenager.

The girl tied her pony to a post. Then she walked up to them and curtsied. "My name is Sybil," she said.

Patrick took a small bow. "I'm Patrick," he said. "And this is my cousin Beth."

Beth gave a little curtsy too.

Sybil reached into the pocket of her apron. She held out a white feather to them. "Would you be in need of a fresh quill?"

Patrick glanced over at Beth. He remembered what Whit had said. "Yes," he said. "And ink as well, please."

Sybil nodded. She put the feather back in her apron pocket. "You both are Patriots then. Are you lookouts?"

"We just got here," Beth said.

"We're looking for Paul Revere," Patrick said. He held out his letter. "We have a letter for him," he added.

"Paul Revere's in Boston," Sybil said. "Indeed, I'm sure of it."

Patrick had no idea where they were. "Is that far?" he asked.

"You wouldn't want to walk there. It's at least seventeen miles from Concord," Sybil said. "You may ride with me to Lexington. After that you can follow the road to Boston."

"Thank you," Beth said.

"In the meantime, will you help with the

cause of freedom?" Sybil asked.

"The cause of freedom?" Beth asked and then looked at Patrick.

"Sure," Patrick said. "If it's for freedom, we'll help."

Beth said, "What can we do?"

"Let me see your apron," Sybil said.

Beth handed her apron to the girl.

Sybil studied it closely. "Good," she said. "The pockets have extra stitching. It will hold the musket balls well enough."

She handed the apron back to Beth. "Tie on your apron and follow me," she said. Then she looked around and lowered her voice. "We're going inside the church. You can both help me collect musket balls today."

"Musket balls?" Beth asked quietly.

"Of course," Sybil said. "All the colonists

are melting down their pewter. They're making musket balls. We're collecting the balls along with other ammunition."

"What does the British army think of that?" Patrick asked.

"It's not for them to know," Sybil said sharply. "We're keeping it all well hidden."

Patrick nodded.

Sybil moved toward the white building. The cousins followed. At the door she said softly, "Be careful inside the building. There are spies everywhere."

"How will we know who is a spy and who isn't?" Beth asked.

Sybil smiled and then said, "Here's what you must do."

Dangerous Spies

"The provincial congress is gathered inside. The men are seated at tables," Sybil said. She took quills from her apron pocket. "First, ask each man if he wants a new quill."

"Quills," Beth said as she took the feathered pens.

"If the man says yes, hand him a quill," Sybil said. "Then move to the next man."

"I get it," Patrick said. "If the first man says yes, then he's a Loyalist."

"A Loyalist?" Beth asked. "Is that someone who is loyal to the king of England?"

"Right," Sybil said. "Whereas a Patriot will reply, 'Yes, and ink as well.'"

"A secret code," Patrick said.

"That's right!" Sybil said. "A Patriot will answer with the secret code. Then you must say, 'The ink will be ready in a minute.' Then hand him a new quill. He will quickly hand you musket balls. Put them in your pockets."

Beth was worried. She hoped she wouldn't get it confused.

Patrick said, "I can hide musket balls in my pockets." He opened his coat. There was a small pocket in the lining. He tucked Paul Revere's letter in it.

Sybil gave him several white quills. He

held them in his fist.

"We'll bring the musket balls out here when we're done," Sybil said. "Then we'll put them in my saddlebags. We'll take them to my uncle. He'll hide them on his property. He's run out of room under his pulpit."

"Under his pulpit?" Beth asked.

"Uncle Jonas is a minister," Sybil said.

"Isn't it against the Constitution to hide gunpowder under a pulpit?" Patrick asked with a smile.

Sybil gazed at him. "What's a constitution?" she asked.

Beth spoke up. "Patrick means the separation of church and state. You know. Aren't ministers and churches supposed to stay out of politics?"

Sybil looked puzzled. "What are you

talking about? Why would ministers stay out of politics?" she asked. "Every minister I know is a Patriot. They all preach about liberty. It's okay to fight for freedom."

Patrick shook his head. "I guess things have changed," he said.

"Changed?" Sybil asked.

"Never mind," Patrick said.

Beth felt excited. Everyone seemed so involved. Even the ministers. Even a teenage girl like Sybil.

Beth and Patrick followed Sybil. They walked through the front entrance of the meetinghouse. She led them down a short flight of stairs. At the bottom was a large room.

Inside, men sat on chairs around small tables. Most of the men wore homemade suits. Their clothes looked like Patrick's outfit. Several men had long white hair tied in short ponytails. Beth guessed that the men were wearing wigs.

One important-looking man sat at a table in front of the others. He fiddled with some papers and held a wood gavel.

The leader cleared his throat and began talking to the men. Beth listened. But she didn't understand because he used long, unfamiliar words. His message seemed to be about being careful while traveling. And he warned the others to avoid the king's men. She assumed he meant *spies*.

The man looked up and saw Sybil. He smiled at her. Sybil curtsied. Beth curtsied too, and Patrick bowed.

"My friends and I have fresh quills for the

men," Sybil said and then added, "With your permission, Mr. Hancock."

Beth took in a quick breath. *Hancock? Is that* the *John Hancock sitting right in front of me?* she wondered.

"Must we endure another interruption, John?" one of the men asked.

"Of course," John Hancock replied. He stood up and hit his gavel on the table.

Bang. Bang. Bang.

"Fresh quills so we may sign this latest proclamation," he announced.

Sybil, Beth, and Patrick went from colonist to colonist with quills.

Beth whispered to the man nearest to her, "Would you like a fresh quill?"

"Yes," he whispered back. "And some ink too." Then the man winked at her.

Beth smiled. "It will be ready in a minute."

She stepped closer and handed a quill to the man. His hand came forward, and she glanced down. He held what looked like small gray marbles. Musket balls.

The man slipped the musket balls into Beth's hand. They were heavy. She slid them into her apron pocket and moved on.

Nobody seemed to notice the exchange.

Beth went to the man at the next table. She asked him in a soft voice, "Would you like a fresh quill?"

"Yes," he said. He picked up his bottle of ink. "And I'm low on ink, too. Do you have any ink?"

Beth felt the heat rise to her cheeks. *He didn't answer in the secret code*, she thought. *Or did he?*

The man frowned at her.

She was struck by fear. *What am I supposed to do?* she wondered.

The Proclamation

Patrick stuffed a handful of musket balls into his pants pocket. He had already filled up the little inside coat pocket. And the larger pockets on the outside.

He looked over at Beth. She was standing next to a table. The wigged man in the seat was scowling at her.

Beth looks scared, Patrick thought. He moved quickly toward her.

Beth gave him a shaky smile.

He asked the man, "Do you need a fresh quill?"

The man turned to him and said, "The young lady already gave me one." He lifted up his jar of ink. "But my ink is low. Do you have any?"

Patrick now understood Beth's expression. *Was this man a Loyalist spy?* he wondered.

Patrick glanced down at the table. The man was writing a letter. Patrick struggled to read the small curly writing. Then he saw a large, handwritten signature: Dr. Benjamin Church.

"We'll see what we can do about more ink, Dr. Church," Patrick said. He touched Beth's elbow. "Move on, Beth."

Beth shot Patrick a look of thanks. She walked to another table.

Patrick moved to the next man. But he kept his eye on Dr. Church.

John Hancock was reading a proclamation to the assembly. "In times as dark as these," he said, "it becomes us, as men and Christians, to—"

Patrick felt his coat pocket move. He looked down. Another man was stuffing musket balls into his pants pocket. Patrick nodded to him and then moved to a different table.

Bang! The sound of a gavel slammed against wood. It echoed like a gunshot. Patrick turned, startled.

"Resolved," John Hancock said loudly. He pounded the table with his gavel again. "This assembly hereby declares a day of public prayer. Let all the good people of this colony seek God together. We set aside for this purpose next Thursday, May 11."

"Hear, hear!" the men said. Several of them pounded the floor with their canes.

Patrick followed their lead. He pounded his cane on the floor too. He marveled that prayer was so important to the colonists. They seemed to understand their need for God's help.

Patrick walked up to John Hancock. "Would you like a fresh quill, sir?" Patrick asked.

John Hancock winked at Patrick and said, "Yes, and some ink too." He pulled open a small drawer in his table. He picked up two handfuls of musket balls.

Patrick put them in his pockets. His pockets were very full. He was afraid they might rip.

Patrick turned to leave.

"That's a fine cane you have," John Hancock said.

"Thank you, sir," Patrick said proudly. "Mr. Whittaker gave it to me."

John Hancock lifted an eyebrow. "Whittaker of Boston?" he asked. "He makes the finest canes in all the colonies. I can't say as much for his inventions, though. He and Ben Franklin get involved in the strangest things. Especially when they're in the same city. Something to do with *kites*. It's more than I care to understand."

Patrick smiled. Whittaker of Boston must have been an ancestor of Mr. Whittaker back home. The letter and the Bible must have originally belonged to him.

Patrick needed to empty his pockets. He looked around the room. Beth was handing out quills. Sybil was giving Dr. Church his new bottle of ink.

Patrick gave a quick bow to John Hancock. Then he hurried from the room. Once outside, he found Sybil's pony. He took a handful of musket balls out of his pocket. He put them into a saddlebag. Then he emptied the rest of his pockets.

He began to put the last handful into the saddlebag. Suddenly, a strong hand grabbed his shoulder.

"Hold on there, young fellow," a man's voice said in his ear. "What's in the saddlebags?"

Patrick cried out and jumped back in fear.

Musket balls fell from his hand. They rolled all over the ground.

Strangers

A tall, thin man held Patrick's shoulder. He wore a tan jacket, brown pants, and brown stockings. He had a large hat.

"Look here, Mr. Brown," he said to another man with him. "We have an arms smuggler."

Patrick felt his stomach twist into a knot. He opened his mouth to speak. But he didn't know what to say.

"To be sure, Ross," said Mr. Brown.

Ross pulled a quill out of his coat pocket.

Then he pulled out a thick wad of papers and a small writing kit. One of the papers looked like a map.

Patrick watched as he wrote something down with a quill. Ross's bony fingers were covered with black ink stains.

Patrick jerked away from Ross. "Leave me alone, or I'll call for help," he said.

"Steady now, young man," Mr. Brown said.

Patrick eyed Mr. Brown carefully. He looked as if he was wearing someone else's clothes. The sleeves on his coat were too long. His brown pants were baggy.

Mr. Brown leaned toward Patrick and said in a low voice, "We're Patriots just like you."

Patrick frowned. Something didn't seem right about these men.

"Tell us, young Patriot," Ross said. "Where

are you taking this ammunition?"

"I'm not sure," Patrick said. He bent over to pick up the musket balls. The letter to Paul Revere slipped out of his pocket. It landed faceup on the ground.

"Are you taking these musket balls to Paul Revere?" Ross asked.

"No," Patrick said. He stuffed the letter back in his pocket. "I don't know where these musket balls are going. The letter is private."

"It's all right, lad," Ross said as he wrote something on his papers.

"What about the cannons?" Mr. Brown asked Ross in a near whisper.

"The boy is being cautious. And so he should be," Ross said to Mr. Brown. "One never knows who to trust these days."

Mr. Brown began to protest. "But—"

"You're doing a good job, lad," Ross said to Patrick. "Carry on."

Patrick stood back up with the musket balls in his hands. "Thank you, sir."

"Come along then," Ross said to Mr. Brown.

Mr. Brown frowned at Patrick and then hitched up his pants.

The two men walked off. They disappeared into the woods behind the building.

Just then, Sybil and Beth came outside. Patrick was relieved. He told the girls about the two men.

"Did you ask them for the secret phrase?" Sybil asked.

"The men told me they were Patriots. Why would I need to ask them about quills?" Patrick asked. He felt annoyed.

"Then you don't know if they were Patriots or not," Sybil said.

"What about the man inside?" Patrick asked. "Dr. Church?"

"What about Dr. Church?" Sybil asked.

Beth's eyes widened. "He didn't know the secret phrase," she said.

Sybil shook her head. "Dr. Church is a leader of the Patriots. He's a close friend of John Hancock and Paul Revere," Sybil said.

"Then someone should make sure he knows the secret code," Beth said. "It was confusing."

"This whole business is confusing," Patrick said as he dropped the last musket balls into the saddlebags. The man called Ross was right. It is hard to know who to trust.

"We have to be careful," Sybil said. She

42

helped Beth put the musket balls into a saddlebag. "If you have any doubt, don't say anything," she added.

Several of the horses stirred. Patrick turned to see the doors of the church meetinghouse swing open.

The men came out. Some got on their horses and galloped off. Others climbed into nearby carriages and rode away.

Sybil pulled herself up on her pony's saddle. "Star is a bit small for the three of us to ride," she said.

"Beth can ride with you," Patrick said. "I'll walk."

"But Lexington is a good six miles from here," Sybil said.

"No problem," Patrick said. He had hiked that far on other adventures.

John Hancock approached them with another man. The Patriot leader waved his gavel in the air. "Carrying such heavy 'quills' all the way to Lexington will make you tired," John Hancock said, smiling broadly. He winked at Patrick.

Patrick smiled back.

John Hancock turned to the other man.

The new man was dressed in shabby clothes. He was short and round. Thick eyebrows almost hid his calm blue eyes.

"What say you, Samuel Adams? Do we have room in our carriage for two more?" John Hancock asked.

"I'll race you!" Sybil said. She dug her heels into Star's sides. She was off like the wind.

"Hurry and climb in," Samuel Adams said. "We can't let that young lady beat us."

He held open the door to a small black carriage. It had a tall roof and white curtains in the windows. Black cushions covered the seats inside. Six horses stood harnessed to the front of it.

Patrick waited while Beth climbed in. John Hancock sat down next to her. Patrick slid into the seat next to Samuel Adams. Patrick held his cane tightly in his hand.

A servant climbed onto the front seat of the carriage. He clicked the reins. "Giddyap!" he shouted. The horses lunged forward at a full gallop.

The race was on.

In the Corncrib

Beth leaned out the carriage window. The horses galloped down the road. She saw Sybil's pony rushing ahead.

Closer and closer they got. Then Sybil shouted, "Faster, Star!" The pony suddenly burst ahead with new speed. They disappeared around a bend.

The carriage finally came to a stop. They were in front of a big house. It was on the edge of a large grassy area. Near the house were several smaller buildings.

Sybil stood nearby holding Star's halter. She smiled at them with a smug look.

A man hurried out of the house. His long white sleeves were puffy. He wore a dark vest over his shirt.

A little girl ran out behind him, followed by an older boy. He looked to be in his teens. More children swarmed around the man. They were like bees buzzing around a hive.

The man playfully shooed them away. He walked over to the carriage.

"Cousin John!" the man shouted.

John Hancock pushed open the carriage door. "Jonas," John Hancock said warmly and climbed out. Beth and Patrick followed. Then Samuel Adams.

The two men shook hands. Reverend

Jonas also greeted Samuel Adams. Then he noticed Beth and Patrick.

"Who are they?" he asked.

"Reverend Jonas Clarke, meet Sybil's new friends," John Hancock said with a sweep of his hand.

"My name is Beth," she said. "And this is my cousin Patrick."

Sybil stepped up to them. "They have a message for Paul Revere," she said.

"Revere is in Boston," Samuel Adams said. "It's getting too dark to ride to Boston now. And too dangerous."

Patrick groaned. Beth saw the frustrated look on his face.

"It's certainly too late for you to leave for Philadelphia," Reverend Clarke said to John Hancock. "You must stay here tonight."

"Thank you, cousin," John Hancock said.

"I offer my thanks as well," Samuel Adams said.

"Does that include everyone?" Sybil asked and pointed to Patrick and Beth.

Reverend Clarke said, "We can squeeze in two more. I'll let my wife know."

The Clarke kids sent up a loud cheer.

"Are all these children yours?" Beth asked. She guessed there were about ten.

"Every last one," Reverend Clarke said.

Reverend Clarke turned to Sybil. "You and your friends can put your collection in the corncrib."

Sybil nodded at Beth and Patrick. "Follow me," she said.

Sybil led Star and the cousins to a small, unpainted shacklike building. Beth thought it looked like a playhouse. But the walls seemed strange. They had boards with open spaces in between them.

Sybil took the saddlebags off Star's saddle. Then she opened the shack door and went inside.

The cousins followed her inside. A pile of dried corncobs filled half the space. Burlap sacks were on the floor.

"Why do the walls have spaces between each board?" Beth asked.

"Don't you know about corncribs?" Sybil asked in surprise. "It's to let the air in and keep the corn dry. Otherwise the corn gets moldy and rotten."

Sybil put the heavy saddlebag on the floor. She opened one of the burlap sacks. A pile of corn sat on top.

"Put as many musket balls as you can into these sacks," she said to Beth and Patrick. "Then cover them up with corn."

When they were done, Sybil led them outside. She shut the door. "We'll need more potatoes for supper," she said.

The cousins followed Sybil around the side of the corncrib. A door lay flat on the ground. Sybil pulled open the door. She led them down the stairs into a dark hole.

Beth thought it was creepy.

"Mind the third step," Sybil said. "The wood's rotten and will break under you."

Beth stepped carefully over the rotten stair. She realized they were going into a cellar. Baskets sat in rows on the floor. They were filled with potatoes, apples, and onions.

Clatter. Clunk. "Oh no. I dropped my

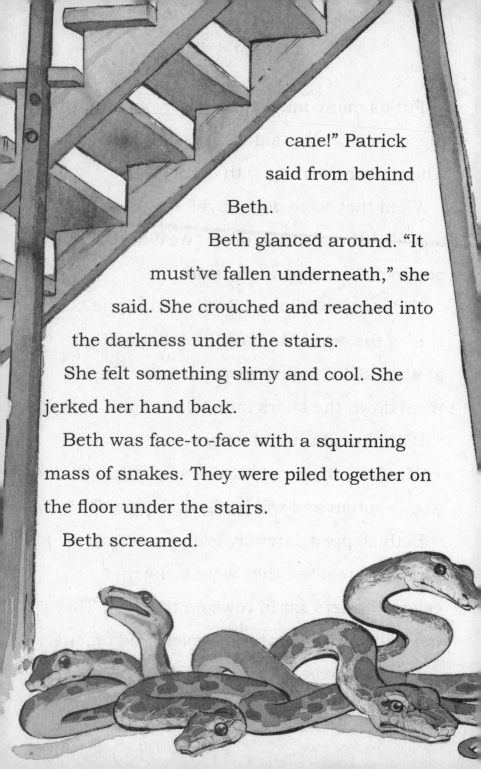

cane!" Patrick said from behind Beth.

Beth glanced around. "It must've fallen underneath," she said. She crouched and reached into the darkness under the stairs.

She felt something slimy and cool. She jerked her hand back.

Beth was face-to-face with a squirming mass of snakes. They were piled together on the floor under the stairs.

Beth screamed.

Alone in the Dark

Sybil rushed over. Patrick clattered down the stairs.

"Pay no mind to them," Sybil said to Beth. "They're black rat snakes. They do no harm."

Beth stepped quickly backward. Patrick stood on tiptoe and tried to see through the shadows.

"Cool!" he said when his eyes adjusted.

"They've been hibernating here all winter," Sybil said. "They're still moving a little slowly."

"Why do you let them stay here?" Beth asked in a shaky voice.

"They keep the rats away," Sybil said.

"Rats?" Beth said.

Sybil nodded. "Some of the rats are as big as cats," she said. "But enough of that. Help me carry potatoes."

Patrick grabbed his cane from the floor near the snakes. Sybil gave the cousins armloads of potatoes. They all carried the potatoes back to the house.

The girls helped prepare supper. Then everyone sat down to eat with the Clarke family. They had a hot meal of potatoes and roast beef.

Soon it was time for bed.

"Patrick can sleep in the stable," Reverend

Clarke said. "He'll be warm enough there."

"Indeed, I'm sure of it," Sybil said. "Beth can sleep in the trundle bed in my room."

Sybil got a quilt. She gave Beth a lantern to carry. Then she led the cousins outside to one of the buildings.

Patrick looked up at the night sky. The darkness was blacker than it was back home. There were no electric streetlights. Instead, thousands of stars twinkled like lights on a Christmas tree.

Patrick's teeth started to chatter. It was a chilly night.

Sybil opened the stable door and took the cousins inside.

John Hancock's carriage was parked in the middle. Horses stood in the stalls on either side of it. Patrick heard one of them stamp its hooves.

Sybil took the lantern from Beth. She hung it on a post. It gave out a small circle of light.

Sybil climbed up a ladder to a loft above. Patrick and Beth climbed up too.

A large pile of loose hay sat on the loft floor. At the back of the loft were stacked piles of hay. They reached almost to the ceiling.

Patrick looked up. The roof rafters were exposed and looked like giant wooden ribs.

Sybil spread out the quilt on the hay.

"This will be a nice soft bed," she said. "You'll get a good night's sleep."

"Can we leave for Boston first thing in the morning?" Patrick asked.

Sybil shook her head. "You can't be going

tomorrow," she said. "Father expects you to join us at our meeting. Tomorrow is Sunday. Nobody travels on Sunday."

"We don't have time to stay another day," Patrick said.

"You'd be stopped and questioned along the way," Sybil said. Then she said good night and climbed down the ladder.

"It'll be all right," Beth said as she climbed down after Sybil.

Sybil took the lantern from the post. She and Beth left the stable.

Now Patrick was all alone. In the dark. He felt his way to the quilt. He sat on it. The hay felt soft underneath.

Patrick stared into the darkness and sighed. This adventure wasn't going the way he thought it would.

A noise broke into his gloomy thoughts.
Pitter patter. Pitter patter.

Mice? he thought. *Or rats. Rats the size of
mountain lions. That's crazy!* He pushed the
image out of his mind.

The noise stopped.

He waited.
Whatever had
caused the noise
was still now.

The sweet smell of
hay soothed him. The heat from the horses
below warmed the stable loft. It was much
warmer inside. He was surprised at how
cozy he felt now.

Patrick took off his jacket. He took the
letter out of his pocket. It was too dark to
see anything.

He put the letter away again and folded his jacket. He placed it beside him on the hay.

He wrapped himself up in the quilt. He closed his eyes.

He thought about the noises around the stable. A snort from one of the horses. A distant hoot from an owl. A barking dog.

Then he thought of the rats again. And the snakes under the stairs.

Patrick didn't like to admit he felt scared. But what if those creatures crawled over him while he slept? That was enough to keep him awake. If only for a few minutes.

Then he fell asleep.

Clang. Clang. Clang.

Patrick sat up with a start. The loud noise sounded as if someone were hitting a pan with a stick.

"Breakfast!" a voice shouted.

Patrick rubbed his eyes. He sat up and yawned. Then he stretched.

His hand brushed against a piece of hay in his hair. He took it out and then shook his head quickly. A few more stray bits fell to the ground.

He reached for his jacket.

That's strange, Patrick thought. The jacket wasn't where he remembered putting it. It was a few feet farther away.

He also thought he had folded his jacket in half. Now it lay flat and spread out.

Patrick stood up and put on the jacket. He buttoned it. One of his buttons was missing.

He reached inside his pocket for Paul Revere's letter.

Where is it? he wondered. *How could it be gone?*

He remembered taking the letter out of the pocket. But he also remembered putting it back. Was he wrong? Had it fallen out when he folded the jacket?

Patrick lifted up the quilt. Nothing. He dug through the hay with his cane. Still nothing.

He checked his pocket again. Empty.

He checked all his pockets. They were empty too.

He climbed down the ladder and looked around. He saw three deep shoe prints in the dirt.

"Patrick!" Beth called from outside.

How was he going to tell her? He'd lost the letter to Paul Revere.

Emergency!

Beth stood at the front door of Reverend Clarke's house. Inside, everyone was rushing back and forth. Mrs. Clarke was busy getting the children ready for church.

"Patrick," Beth shouted again. "Breakfast!"

She looked across the large grassy area. Sybil had told her it was called Lexington Green. Beth noticed big buildings on the other side.

The stable door opened. Patrick appeared.

Beth thought Patrick's face looked pale. He was either sick or worried. Maybe both.

Sybil came up behind Beth.

"We must hurry, or we'll be late for meeting," Sybil said.

"Come on!" Beth shouted as she waved at Patrick.

He waved back to Beth and ran to her. By then his face had turned red. "I've got to tell you something—in private," he said.

"There's no time now," Beth said. "We're about to eat breakfast." She gave him a small smile and turned toward the house.

She and Patrick walked inside.

Beth went to the kitchen area to help. She scooped hot oatmeal out of a pot. She put it into heavy pewter bowls. There were a lot of children to feed!

Beth joined the crowd around the table.

Patrick sat with the men. Reverend Clarke stood and prayed.

He sat down again when he finished the prayer. Everyone began to eat their warm oatmeal and lumps of cheese.

Beth forgot about Patrick after breakfast. Again she was too busy to talk to him. There were hair ribbons to tie. And old-fashioned shoes to button.

Later, one of the children banged on a pan. Everyone gathered and made their way to the Lexington meetinghouse.

Beth came alongside Patrick to walk across the green. But she couldn't talk to him to find out what was wrong. They were surrounded by Clarke children. Patrick even let one small boy climb on his shoulders.

They made their way inside the square gray meetinghouse. Wooden risers were arranged in rows facing a podium. Beth sat down on a seat and sighed with relief. Unfortunately, Patrick sat across the aisle from Beth.

We'll just have to wait, she thought. *I hope the sermon isn't too long.*

Reverend Clarke walked up to the pulpit. He wore a long black robe. Beth thought he looked like a judge.

Reverend Clarke preached about the power of God over governments. He said that Christians are in His hands. God knows when we suffer. He sees the cruel hand of King George. We must be grateful when times are good. And we must remember that God is present in bad times.

Beth felt her heart stir with pride for her country. But Beth's teacher at school wouldn't have liked it. She said talking about politics in church was un-American.

No one here would agree with that! Beth thought. Not Reverend Clarke or his large family. Not John Hancock or Samuel Adams, who sat nearby. Not the little children or the teenagers. Not even the people older than her grandma.

For these people, freedom was something God gave them. They weren't going to let a king take it away.

This is how America started, Beth thought. *Christians are involved. Churches are involved. For freedom. For liberty. For America.*

Reverend Clarke pounded on the pulpit.

Beth suddenly remembered what Sybil had said about gunpowder. It was stored underneath the pulpit. She wondered if it could blow up when Reverend Clarke pounded. She hoped not.

Reverend Clarke paused and lifted his head as if he heard something. Beth heard a clatter of hooves coming from outside. All eyes went to the windows facing the road. A man galloped toward the meetinghouse.

"It's Paul Revere!" someone whispered. "Something must be wrong!"

10

The Search

Reverend Clarke stepped away from the pulpit. "The meeting will be dismissed," he said. "You may leave in order and quiet."

Everyone stood up. Beth hurried over to Patrick.

"You can give Paul Revere the letter," she said to him.

Patrick frowned and shook his head. "That's what I wanted to tell you," he said. "I can't find the letter."

Beth winced. "You lost it?" she asked.

"I don't know," Patrick said. "When I woke up this morning, it was gone."

"Did you drop it in the carriage? Or maybe it's in the corncrib," Beth said.

"It was in my jacket pocket before I went to sleep," Patrick said.

Everyone was now outside with Paul Revere. Beth and Patrick were alone.

"How could it just disappear?" Beth asked.

"I think someone stole it," Patrick said.

"Who? Only Sybil and I knew you had it," Beth said.

Patrick shook his head. "*And* the two strangers. They saw me put the musket balls into the saddlebags," he said.

"You showed it to them?" Beth asked.

Patrick shook his head again. "It fell out of

my pocket," he said. "I know they saw it."

"You think they followed you back to the house?" Beth asked. "And that they sneaked into the stable last night to steal it?"

Beth thought it sounded like a wild idea.

"Yes," Patrick said. But he didn't sound as sure as he had a moment ago.

"We'll run back to Reverend Clarke's home," Beth suggested. "We'll search again."

"It won't be there," Patrick insisted. "Those two men stole it."

"Let's look again," Beth said. "Then we'll be sure."

Patrick looked at her and then nodded. "You're right," he said. "Let's go."

Beth and Patrick hurried out the door. The crowd of people pressed around a man standing next to a horse. Beth guessed it was Paul Revere. She and Patrick needed to find that letter *fast*.

They ran back to Reverend Clarke's house. Patrick hurried away from Beth and ran toward the stable. "I'll check the stable again," he shouted. "You check the house."

Beth ran through the front doorway. She headed straight for the round dining table.

First she pulled out the chair where Patrick sat that morning. Next she looked where she thought he'd sat the night before. Then she bent down to look underneath the table.

She heard a sudden noise behind her. Beth whirled around and looked toward a window. A man stood half hidden behind the long curtains.

Beth let out a shriek.

The man stepped out. He held on to his belt. Beth wondered if he thought his trousers might fall.

"Did you lose something?" he asked in a low voice.

"Who are you?" she asked. "What are you doing here?"

"It's no business of yours," the man said.

Beth made a sudden rush for the front door.

The man moved quickly. He grabbed her arm and then let out a small laugh.

Beth stomped on his foot and twisted free. He grabbed for her again. She dodged him and moved behind the dining table.

The man muttered under his breath. Then he threw himself across the top of the table. Beth scrambled underneath it.

Beth pushed past the chairs. She half crawled and half ran for the door. She lifted the latch and pulled it open.

The man came up behind her. But she was faster. She sprang toward the stretch of grass ahead.

Beth raced in the direction of the corncrib. She had an idea.

The man started after her, but she heard him grunt loudly. She glanced back and saw that he'd slipped and fallen. She raced around the corncrib. She came to the cellar door in the ground.

She grabbed the door handle and pulled up as hard as she could. The door didn't budge.

The man was coming toward her. She took the handle with both hands. She gave the door a mighty heave. This time it flew open.

She scampered down the cellar stairs. She took care to skip the third step. She reached the bottom and stopped. She turned around and looked up at the door frame.

The man came into view. His face was twisted in a sneer. He was red-faced and puffing loudly. "Now . . . I've . . . got you," he said between breaths.

He hitched up his pants with his hand. Then he took a step. And a second. He kept his eyes on Beth as he reached up and

straightened his hat.

Then he put his foot on the third step.

Crack!

The wooden step broke under his weight.

"Aaah!" he cried out as his leg fell through the step. He waved his hands in the air.

His other leg was still on the second step. His weight broke that step as well. He disappeared below the wooden staircase.

"I've hurt my leg!" the man shouted. Then he gave a little cry. "What's this?" he called out.

Hiss-ss! Hiss-ss!

"Snakes!" the man shouted.

Beth could hear the man thrashing

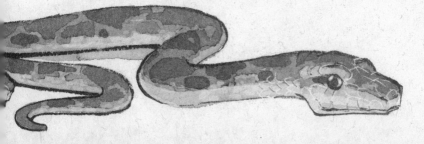

around. Then he let out a long howl.

Beth didn't wait to find out what happened next. She raced up the stairs as fast as she could. She leaped over the broken steps to the outside.

Bony Fingers

Patrick searched the stable again. He checked inside the carriage. Nothing. He climbed up the ladder to the loft. He used his cane to spread the hay. Nothing.

Patrick climbed down the ladder again. He saw the three deep footprints in the mud. He had assumed they were his and Beth's and Sybil's. They had all been in the stable the night before.

Patrick placed his foot over one of the

footprints. It was too large for his foot. And it was too large for the girls' feet.

"The men *were* here!" he said to himself.

Patrick heard a bang at the far end of the stable. A tall, thin man stepped out from the shadows. It was one of the men who'd questioned him outside the white church. Patrick remembered his name was Ross.

Ross held a pitchfork and walked toward Patrick.

"Tell me where the musket balls are," he said, "or I'll run you through." He shook the pitchfork at Patrick.

Patrick thought about running for the door. But he was afraid Ross would catch him. So he climbed the ladder.

Ross dropped the pitchfork and came after him. The tall man shook the ladder as he climbed.

Patrick reached the top of the ladder. He stepped onto the loft. He turned and saw two hands with bony fingers gripping the top rung. Ross's face came into view.

"Where's my letter?" Patrick demanded.

Ross took one hand off the ladder. He opened his coat flap. "I don't have it," Ross said. "Come look inside my coat."

Patrick came a few steps closer.

Ross suddenly reached forward to grab his leg. Patrick stepped back and stumbled over a mound of hay. Ross climbed the rest of the way up the ladder. He clenched his fists as he stood in front of Patrick.

Patrick pushed himself farther back into the loft. He swung his cane wildly at Ross. The man easily sidestepped it. Patrick backed into a pile of hay.

Patrick spun around and climbed up the piles of hay. If only he could get to the top. Then he could climb into the rafters.

Suddenly Patrick felt Ross's strong hand grab his right ankle.

"No!" Patrick shouted and kicked hard. His leg came free.

He continued his climb to the top.

But Ross clawed his way upward too. He was tossing handfuls of hay out of the way.

The stack of hay began to shrink. Ross was getting closer.

Patrick heard Ross sneeze. The hay must have tickled his nose. The sneeze made Ross jerk backward.

He slid down the stack.

Patrick jumped, tumbling down the stack

on the other side of Ross. He fell into the corner of the loft floor. The boards groaned and came loose as he landed on them.

Patrick felt dazed. He clutched his cane and looked for Ross. A cloud of dust made it hard for Patrick to see.

Ross had fallen back toward the ladder. He was getting to his feet again.

Patrick was truly cornered. He could tell that Ross saw it too. The man grunted with a look of satisfaction and stood up.

Patrick was lying flat on the floor and spotted a loose board. He thought he might use it as a shield. He yanked up the board, and two more came with it.

The missing boards left a large opening. It looked large enough for him to slip through.

Ross must have noticed the opening too.

He rushed at Patrick.

Patrick lowered himself through the hole feet first. He prayed he wouldn't land on anything pointed.

He fell into a pile of old hay and compost.

Squeak! Squeak!

Rats exploded out of the pile. They ran everywhere. A rat as big as a cat scampered over Patrick's leg.

A terrible smell engulfed Patrick like a cloud. His eyes watered from the odor of rotting food and dung.

He looked up. Ross peered at him through the hole above.

"I'll get you," Ross said through clenched teeth. Then he disappeared from view.

Patrick guessed he was headed for the ladder.

Patrick crawled to his feet. His hand rested against something small and hard. Then he realized it was the brass button from his coat! He put it in his pocket.

Then Patrick flung himself at the stable door. It burst open, and he nearly ran into Beth.

"Patrick!" Beth shouted. "I caught the spy! He's in the snake pit!"

Patrick now heard cries of "Help me!" from the direction of the cellar.

Just then Patrick heard Ross inside the stable.

"Come on!" Patrick shouted as he grabbed Beth's arm. He pulled her along with him.

The cousins raced to the front of the house. The crowd from the meetinghouse was coming down the road. Paul Revere was with them on his horse.

"We're rescued!" Patrick said. He
swallowed hard as he tried to catch his
breath. He glanced back in time to see Ross
moving toward the cellar door.

"Look," Patrick said, pointing toward the
cellar.

Beth followed his gaze. "I hope there's no
more of them," Beth said.

"Just two," Patrick said. "And they won't
get away."

Patrick stepped away from Beth. He
waved his cane at the coming crowd. "Hurry!
Spies! We found spies!" he shouted.

Everyone on the road stared at him. At
first they looked puzzled. Then the men
began to walk quickly. Then they broke into
a full run.

"We'll lead them to the cellar," Patrick said to Beth. He raced ahead of her to the cellar door. All was dark below.

John Hancock and Samuel Adams hurried to Patrick's side. Paul Revere and the others followed.

"They're in there," Patrick said. "Two of them."

"Come out!" John Hancock commanded.

Nothing happened.

"Come out, or we'll tar and feather you," Samuel Adams called.

"They couldn't escape that fast," Patrick said.

John Hancock shouted again for the men to come out.

Ross appeared in the dim light below. Then Mr. Brown. They climbed slowly up the stairs and into the daylight.

Mr. Brown was no longer wearing a hat. His long hair was tangled. He moved with a limp. His stockings were torn and dirty with soil and blood.

"Explain yourselves," John Hancock said.

"What are you doing on the Reverend Clarke's property?" Samuel Adams asked. His eyes narrowed. "You look like troublemakers. Start talking, or we'll start boiling the tar."

"We're not spies," Mr. Brown said.

"I'll wager that these two children are the spies," Ross said. He pointed a bony finger at Patrick. "I found the boy searching the stable."

"The girl was searching the house," Mr. Brown said.

"We're not spies!" Patrick said. "They're the

spies. They're lying!"

"Why would you be here alone during meeting time?" Ross asked sharply. "Looking for weapons? Stores of ammunition? Important papers? What else were we to think? The Loyalists often use children to do their dirty work!"

Mr. Brown waved a hand at Patrick and Beth. "There's no doubt about it. They're the spies and traitors!"

Oh, Rats!

Patrick was angry. *They're lying!* he thought as he clenched his fists.

"We'll get to the bottom of this," Samuel Adams said. He stepped forward. "There are ways to expose the real traitors."

"Come to the house," Reverend Clarke said. Then he turned to an older child and said, "Please take your younger siblings off to play somewhere. We need privacy."

The adults moved inside with Beth and

Patrick. John Hancock stood at the head of the dining table. Reverend Clarke stood next to him. Samuel Adams and Paul Revere took seats nearby.

"Sit there," John Hancock said to Patrick and Beth. He pointed to two chairs to the left of the table. Patrick and Beth obeyed. Sybil stood behind them.

"And you men sit there," John Hancock said. He pointed at two chairs to the right of the table. Mr. Brown hitched up his pants and sat down next to Ross.

John Hancock pulled his gavel out of his pocket. *Bang. Bang. Bang.* "Speak first, you men," he said. "You're strangers to us. State your business here."

Mr. Brown spoke first. "We came from Boston yesterday to join the Patriots."

"You came from Boston?" Paul Revere asked. "Who told you to come to this house?"

"Whittaker, the cane maker," Mr. Brown said.

Patrick nearly leaped from his chair. "Mr. Whittaker sent *us*," he shouted. "He gave me this cane!"

"Sit down, boy," John Hancock said firmly.

Patrick sat down. His face was red with anger and embarrassment.

Mr. Brown cleared his throat and said, "Whittaker also said the Loyalists were using children as spies."

Patrick was ready to protest again. But Beth put a hand on his arm. "It'll be okay," she whispered to him.

Patrick leaned back and shoved his hands into his pants pockets. He felt helpless. His fingers brushed against the button he'd found in the stable.

"We spoke to the boy yesterday," the man called Ross said. "He was acting suspiciously and carrying musket balls."

"Patrick was helping us," Sybil said.

"Sybil, how long have you known this boy and girl?" John Hancock asked.

"I met them only yesterday," Sybil said.

John Hancock pointed his gavel at Patrick and Beth. "So, no one has ever seen you before yesterday. Where are you from? Where are your parents?"

Patrick looked at Beth. She gazed at him helplessly. What could he say? Would they listen to the truth about Mr. Whittaker's Imagination Station?

Patrick's fingers moved around the button in his pocket.

My button! Patrick suddenly thought. An idea formed in Patrick's head.

"Sir," Patrick said to John Hancock, "all the evidence I need is in the stable. May I go and get it?"

"How do I know you won't run away?" John Hancock asked.

"I'll go with him," Samuel Adams said. "I'll throttle him if he tries to run away."

Patrick scraped his chair backward. He ran out the door, across the grass, and into the stable. Mr. Adams followed him.

Patrick headed to the back corner of the stable.

"What are you up to?" Samuel Adams asked from behind him.

Patrick picked up a large rock. He threw it at the pile of hay and compost. A dozen rats raced away.

"This had better be worth it, boy," Samuel Adams said. "That's one foul-smelling heap."

Patrick used his cane to dig through the smelly nest.

"It's where I found my missing button," Patrick told Samuel Adams. "If the rats took my button, then they must have—"

Just then he saw the letter to Paul Revere. He knelt down and carefully picked it up. A corner had been nibbled off. "This is the letter Mr. Whittaker gave me to deliver. Look, it's still sealed."

"So it is," Samuel Adams said. "We had better deliver it."

Patrick and Samuel Adams returned to the house. Patrick handed the letter to Paul Revere. Paul Revere looked at the letter. Then he sniffed it and frowned.

"I thought these two men stole the letter from me," Patrick said as Paul Revere opened it.

All eyes were on Paul Revere. He read the letter silently to himself. Then he looked up and whispered to John Hancock. He pointed to a section of the letter.

John Hancock nodded. Then he turned to Mr. Brown and Ross. "You will come quietly or face the consequences," he said.

The two spies looked as if they were going to flee. Reverend Clarke and Samuel Adams moved next to them. Samuel Adams now had a small pistol in his hand.

"Take them away!" John Hancock said. "Tie them up for now."

"How dare you!" Mr. Brown shouted. "What evidence do you have against us?"

Paul Revere waved the letter in the air. "This is from my friend Whittaker in Boston. He's the very man you claimed sent you," he said. "You visited him to seek information about us. He knew you as Loyalists the moment he set eyes on you."

"He's wrong!" Ross shouted. "Why would he think we were spies?"

"Because he saw you both in Boston," Paul Revere said. "You were chatting to a British captain and wearing Army redcoats."

"He was mistaken!" Mr. Brown said.

"Mr. Whittaker is never mistaken," John Hancock said. "He sees everything and everyone in Boston."

Patrick suddenly remembered another detail. "Check his pockets, Mr. Adams," he said. "That one called Ross has some papers."

"Turn out your pockets," Samuel Adams said to Ross.

The man obeyed. There was nothing but a few coins.

"You forgot one," Beth said and pointed to the inside of Ross's coat.

John Hancock didn't move. Mr. Adams pushed the coat aside. He pulled out a wad of paper. He glanced through the pages.

"Hand-drawn maps, names, addresses . . ." Samuel Adams said. "We need to burn these."

"Make certain the two men are locked up well," John Hancock said.

Reverend Clarke called his oldest son.

They took the two spies away.

Paul Revere slipped the letter into his pocket.

John Hancock gazed at Patrick and Beth. "Thank you for being patient while we looked into the matter," he said. "One never knows whom to trust these days."

"That's what Ross told me," Patrick said.

John Hancock turned to Paul Revere and said, "You didn't come all the way from Boston to catch spies. Why are you here?"

"And why have you ridden on the Lord's Day?" Sybil asked.

Paul Revere looked at John Hancock and Samuel Adams. "I have come for you and Sam," he said. "You are both now in great danger. You must flee, I tell you. Or you'll be hanged."

Willing to Die

Beth looked at John Hancock and Samuel Adams. They seemed stunned by the news.

"Explain yourself," Samuel Adams said.

Paul Revere moved around the table. "The British officers know you are Patriot leaders."

Beth gave a little gasp. The men were in great danger. The British were after them.

Paul Revere said, "The British believe you have important documents. Those documents show where the militia's weapons and ammunition are stored."

John Hancock and Samuel Adams looked at each other.

"If they capture you, they can hang you for treason," Paul Revere said. "*And* they'll ruin our means to fight."

"When will they take action?" Samuel Adams asked.

"Soon," said Paul Revere. "They're up to something. A number of small boats with British soldiers were launched last night. The boats have been positioned close to the men-of-war."

"Men-of-war?" Patrick asked. "Do you mean more soldiers?"

"Not soldiers," Samuel Adams said. "*Battleships*. They carry cannons powerful enough to destroy a fort."

"I must get back to Boston," Paul Revere said. "Be warned. Hide our weapons and any important papers you have."

Everyone said good-bye. Paul Revere left. Beth heard his horse's hooves clomp away.

The other men made plans. "First," Samuel Adams said, "someone needs to watch over Mr. Hancock's carriage in the stable."

Patrick volunteered to guard it. Beth felt proud of her cousin.

Then Reverend Clarke returned. "I suspect we'll have a busy day tomorrow," he said.

"Good," Samuel Adams said to Patrick. "You'll sound the alarm if someone tries to look inside it. We can hide it in the woods tomorrow."

"And the spies?" asked John Hancock.

"Tied up and locked in the cellar," replied Reverend Clarke. "I hope they like snakes and potatoes!"

The rest of the day was quiet. Then everyone went to bed. Beth said good night to Patrick. She stood at the front door and watched him. He walked through the dark toward the stable.

Just then Beth heard a loud bang from around the house. Patrick must have heard it too. He changed direction to follow the noise. Beth ran after him.

They both reached the cellar door at the same time. It was lying open.

A twig snapped farther away near the woods.

Beth gasped. Two large shadows were

disappearing into the trees.

"The spies!" she shouted. "They've escaped!"

Beth's shouts brought the house to life. Reverend Clarke ran to the front door. He began barking orders to his older boys. "Go to the tavern and find the landlord, John Buckman," he commanded. "Call out the minutemen to search for the spies. Tell Hancock we need more men to guard this house."

Clarke's oldest son signaled two of his brothers. Then off they raced toward the tavern.

Reverend Clarke waved to Patrick. "It'll be safer if you spend the night in the kitchen," he said. "We'll trust God to watch John

Hancock's carriage."

Patrick was relieved. Fear of rats was bad enough. But fear of the British spies would've kept him awake all night.

Patrick lay on the hard wood floor of the kitchen. He stared at the ceiling. He listened to bumps, thuds, and soft grunts.

Some men patrolled outside the house so everyone could sleep safely.

The next two days went by quickly. Patrick and Beth joined in the work around town. The cousins moved the ammunition and supplies to safer places.

The Clarke children hid the carriage in the woods and moved important papers to the tavern.

Patrick was surprised at the clever places the Clarkes found to hide weapons.

He saw Patriots stash musket balls in the hollows of trees. Small packets of gunpowder were hidden in kitchen pots. Then the pots were topped off with grain and flour.

Patrick helped bury muskets in boxes. Or hide them behind false walls in houses. He helped bury boxes of firearms under farm crops.

Patrick and Beth returned to the Clarke's house at the end of each day.

At the end of the second day, they walked around to the back of the house and found Sybil. She smiled at them as she dismounted Star. Next to her was a tall brown horse. Its mane was jet black.

Patrick heard drums beating in the distance. *Rat-a-tat-tat.*

They reached Sybil and she said,

"Something's happened."

Sybil raced around to the front of the house. Patrick and Beth followed.

They both stopped when they saw the reason for the beating drum. On Lexington Green men marched and drilled to its tapping. Each man wore a triangle-shaped hat and held a musket.

Patrick watched the drills. His heart pounded with pride and fear.

Old and young men marched. They were Patriots practicing

to fight for their freedom. They were going to take up arms. They would fight against the king's soldiers who were oppressing them. They were willing to die for what they believed in.

Beth stood at Patrick's side.

"What's today's date?" he asked her.

"I don't know exactly," she said. "Sometime in April 1775. Why?"

"I think we're watching the warm-up for battle," Patrick said. "Remember the Battles of Lexington and Concord?"

Beth gasped. "Something happened before that," she said.

"What?" Patrick asked.

"Paul Revere's ride," she said.

A Dangerous Ride

At bedtime, Beth was tired—and bothered. She knew it was a night that would go down in history. Paul Revere would make his famous ride.

Snippets of a poem ran through her head. But she could only remember a few words: "One if by land and two if by sea . . ."

Patrick was no help. He couldn't remember what had happened or when.

The whole house was abuzz with activity.

There was too much noise for Reverend Clarke's younger children to sleep. He and Mrs. Clarke had a hard time getting them to stay in bed. The adults spoke in low voices between themselves.

Beth lay in bed. She was sure she wouldn't be able to sleep. Yet a sudden sound woke her up. *Rat-a-tat-tat.* Somewhere outside a drum banged out a loud beat.

Beth sat up in bed. She didn't know what time it was.

Clang. Clang. Clang. A bell started to ring.

Bang! Bang! Bang! Someone knocked on the front door.

Footsteps pounded on the floorboards in the halls. Doors slammed.

"Let's find out what's happening," Sybil said in the darkness.

Beth jumped out of bed.

The girls reached the ground floor.

Paul Revere stood next to the dining table. He was talking with John Hancock, Samuel Adams, and Reverend Clarke. He wore a triangle hat and a long, heavy black coat. His thick boots were spattered with mud.

What's he doing here? Beth wondered. *Isn't he supposed to be out riding around the countryside? Or did he start his ride from here?*

Beth and Sybil joined the men. Patrick came in too. His hair was messed up. And his eyes looked puffy from sleeping.

"It's not safe for you to stay here," Paul Revere said to John Hancock and Samuel Adams. "The redcoats are marching this way. They have orders to arrest both of you.

And they'll take our supplies."

Patrick said, "We moved a lot of supplies out to Concord today."

Paul Revere nodded. "I'll ride on to Concord, then. I'll rouse the countryside."

The men each shook his hand. "Be careful, Paul," John Hancock said.

Paul Revere touched the tip of his hat and then left.

John Hancock and Samuel Adams began to discuss whether to leave. John Hancock wanted to stay and fight the British.

Reverend Clarke insisted that both men were key leaders. They needed to live so they could build a new nation.

The debate continued.

Reverend Clarke leaned over a hand-drawn map. John Hancock and Samuel Adams studied it closely.

Suddenly there was a loud crash. Beth and Patrick ran down the hallway. They reached the front door as Paul Revere rushed inside.

"Paul! What are you doing here?" Reverend Clarke shouted.

"I never made it to Concord. British soldiers stopped me," Paul Revere said. He was breathing hard. "They took my horse."

Then he saw John Hancock and Samuel Adams. "Why are you still here?" Paul asked. "The redcoats are coming this way!"

"It's no longer a point of debate," John Hancock said. He gestured to Samuel Adams. The two men prepared to leave.

Patrick had helped Reverend Clarke's sons hide the carriage in the woods. They hurried to the hiding place and brought it back to the farm. Paul Revere left them and headed to the tavern. He went to get the trunk and the important papers.

By then it was getting close to dawn. The cousins and Sybil gathered again in front of the house.

Lexington Green was crowded with minutemen. The drummer was still drumming. The bell was still ringing.

"If Paul Revere never made it to Concord," Beth said, "who will warn the townspeople?"

Beth looked at Sybil and then Patrick.

"We can ride to Concord," Sybil said. She gathered up her long skirt and ran toward the stable. "I'll saddle up the horses. They'll be ready in a minute."

15

War!

Patrick and Beth ran after Sybil.

Sybil saddled Star. Then she went to the second horse. She patted its black mane. "I hope you're ready to ride fast, Sugar," she said.

Patrick leaned his cane against a post. Then he helped Sybil saddle Sugar. He gave Beth a leg up onto the saddle. She scooted back so he could climb up.

"What about your cane?" Beth asked.

"I don't need it now," Patrick said. He settled into the saddle in front of Beth.

"How will a cane help me on a ride?" Patrick asked.

"We must go!" Sybil shouted. She was on Star now.

"You have to bring the cane," Beth said. "Please! Mr. Whittaker said to always keep it with you."

Patrick groaned. "Oh, all right," he said. He climbed down and grabbed the cane. Then he pulled himself back up on the saddle.

"Satisfied?" he asked smugly. He flicked the reins. "Let's go!"

Star and Sugar trotted out through the stable doors.

They now faced the green. The soldiers in

red and the Patriots had their rifles raised.

"This way!" Sybil shouted. She raced away from the green.

Patrick urged Sugar to follow. Beth wrapped her arms around Patrick's waist.

Gunshots exploded behind them.

Pow! Pow! Bang! Bang! Bang!

Patrick glanced back. Clouds of white and black smoke covered both groups of soldiers. Patrick couldn't see what was happening. But he knew many Patriots would die.

Patrick dug his heels into Sugar's side. They galloped faster after Sybil and Star.

The early morning air was cool. The gray predawn light shone on the road in front of them. Patrick could hear the twitter of birds waking up in the trees.

They came to a group of houses. This
village was quiet and still.

They trotted alongside Sybil and Star.

"You ride down that street," Sybil said,
pointing to the right. "I'll ride down this one.
We'll meet on the other end where they join
up again."

They reached the first house. Patrick
pulled on Sugar's reins.

"Whoa," he said.

"The redcoats are coming!" Beth
shouted.

Her voice

sounded small. The morning chorus of birds seemed louder. No one in the house stirred.

"The redcoats are coming!" Patrick shouted at the top of his voice.

Everything was still.

"People are still asleep," Beth said. "We have to go door to door to wake them up."

Patrick looked at the houses. Doors and fences lined the front of each one.

"That will take forever," he said.

"What can we do?"" Beth asked.

Patrick felt angry. He lifted his cane. He felt like throwing it through someone's window. *That would wake them up*, he thought. Then he had an idea.

He tugged at the reins. Sugar moved closer to the fence.

"What are you doing?" Beth asked.

Patrick swung the cane against the
wooden fence. *Bang! Bang! Bang!*

A window opened from upstairs. A man
leaned out the window. He was wearing a
white nightcap on his head.

"What the blazes!" he shouted.

"The redcoats are coming!" Patrick and
Beth shouted at the same time.

The man looked startled and then waved
his hand. "Alert the others!" he cried.

"Giddyap!" Patrick shouted to Sugar. They
moved to the next house. The door was a
couple of feet from the street.

Patrick used the cane to hammer the door.
Again a man appeared in the second-story
window. The cousins shouted their message.

Then they were off down the road. The
big horse galloped past each house. Patrick

rapped on the doors or fences with his cane.

He and Beth took turns shouting, "The redcoats are coming! The redcoats are coming!"

Soon, candles glowed from inside all the houses. Men and women stepped outside into the cool morning air.

The cousins reached the end of the street. Sybil rode up to meet them on Star. They exchanged smiles and nods, and then they raced on.

By now the sky was a cotton-candy pink.

They galloped until they reached another group of houses. Men with red coats and muskets stepped onto the street. They formed a line to block the road.

Sybil and Patrick brought their horses to a halt. One of the redcoats broke through the line. He pointed to Patrick.

"I know these children," the man shouted.
"They're Patriots and a nuisance! Stop them!"

"It's Mr. Brown," Beth cried.

"Hold on!" Patrick called over his shoulder.

Patrick kicked his heels into Sugar's sides.
The horse reared. Then it galloped to an
alley on the right. Sybil raced along behind
them on Star.

Patrick's heart beat fast. He looked
down a narrow lane. A handful of redcoats
appeared at the end. All of them carried
muskets. Drums beat somewhere.

"Oh no!" Beth called out.

Patrick urged Sugar to go faster.

They reached another road. Patrick stole
a quick look back toward the town. The
line of redcoats they'd met earlier was still

there. An officer on horseback seemed to be shouting at the soldiers.

Patrick looked forward. He saw a large town just beyond a bridge.

"Concord!" Sybil shouted at them.

Concord! Patrick thought with relief. *We've made it all the way to Concord. This is where the Imagination Station first landed.*

Sugar and Star pounded across the bridge into Concord. Beth shouted out the warning. Patrick used his cane to make as much noise as possible. The men and women of the town rushed into the streets.

"The redcoats are across the bridge!" Patrick called out. His throat began to hurt.

They reached the other side of Concord. The horses slowed to a trot.

"What now?" Patrick asked Sybil.

"We've done as much as we can," Sybil
said.

They turned their horses and looked
back on the town. A group of colonists were
gathering with their guns. More and more
men joined them.

Just then Patrick heard a familiar hum.
It came from behind a tree beside the road.
He slid down from Sugar's saddle and stood
on wobbly legs. He could see that Beth also
heard the noise. He helped her down. Then
he handed Sugar's reins to Sybil.

"I'm so glad we're leaving," Beth said to
Patrick. "I don't want to see anyone die."

Patrick understood what she meant.
There would be bloodshed and death. This
was where the real war for freedom began.

"We'll go home a different way," Patrick

told Sybil. "But you'd better hurry! Before they start shooting here, too."

"Are you sure you'll be safe?" Sybil asked them.

"We'll be safe enough," Patrick said.

Sybil smiled. "I've no need to worry about you two," she said.

She jabbed her heels into Star's sides. The pony moved slowly forward. She pulled on Sugar's reins. The two horses moved off across a field.

"Good-bye!" Sybil shouted.

"Good-bye!" Beth and Patrick said. They both waved.

The cousins walked into the woods toward the humming noise. The Imagination Station stood in a small clearing with its doors open.

"I'm tired," Beth said.

"So am I," Patrick said. "I'll be glad to get back."

Suddenly, a group of redcoats stepped out from behind the trees.

"The traitors!" a voice called out. It was Ross, the spy. He pointed his musket at them.

Patrick and Beth dove into the machine.

The doors slid shut.

Ka-pow!

The front window of the Imagination Station cracked.

Beth screamed.

A musket ball was stuck in the center of the glass. Cracks in the glass spread out in a circle.

Patrick slapped his palm on the red button.

Everything went dark.

Patrick felt strange. The machine rocked back and forth from side to side. Then it rocked from front to back.

"What's happening?" Beth asked. Her voice was shaking.

The Imagination Station shuddered and rattled. It sounded as if it was falling apart. Beth grabbed Patrick's hand. Patrick closed his eyes tight.

The noise stopped, and the rocking of the machine slowed down. Patrick felt as if they were floating. They moved up and down like ocean waves. He opened his eyes.

Beth still held his hand.

Patrick frowned as he blinked in the darkness. He no longer sat on the cushions in the Imagination Station. He was sitting on something hard and wooden. He felt

pinpricks in his back like small splinters.

They were sitting on the deck of a ship. Their backs were pressed against a tall mast. Patrick looked up at the mast through the dark shadows of the night. The moon shone on a flag flying high in the breeze. He could see a snake against a yellow background. Across the bottom were the words "Don't Tread on Me."

Patrick had seen the symbol before in a history book. "That's an American flag from the Revolutionary War," he said to Beth.

The ship rocked back and forth in the waves. It creaked each time it moved.

Beth let go of Patrick's hand and slowly stood up. "Why didn't we go back to Whit's

End?" she asked.

Patrick wondered if the gunshot had damaged the Imagination Station. He got to his feet. But his legs ached. He grabbed the mast to steady himself.

"We must have landed somewhere in the middle of the war," Patrick said.

"Then why is it so quiet?" Beth asked.

A shadow moved in the darkness behind them. Patrick felt something small and hard push into his back.

A pistol? he wondered.

"Who goes there?" a low voice asked.

To find out more about the next book, *Captured on the High Seas*, visit TheImaginationStation.com.

Cousins Patrick and Beth have landed on the *Royal Louis* in the middle of the Revolutionary War. Cannonballs fly and swords clash—but the *Royal Louis* still falls to the enemy. Will the cousins' new friend, James Forten, be sold into the British slave trade? Will Beth and Patrick lose their freedom while trying to gain it for others? Journey back to 1781, and experience thrilling danger, mystery, and high seas adventure.

Secret Word Puzzle

The founders of the United States chose a motto for their new country. Want to know what it was? Fill in the code on the next page using the code cracker below. The letters in boxes, when written in numbered order, spell out another name for the redcoats.

A = X	J = G	S = P
B = Y	K = H	T = Q
C = Z	L = I	U = R
D = A	M = J	V = S
E = B	N = K	W = T
F = C	O = L	X = U
G = D	P = M	Y = V
H = E	Q = N	Z = W
I = F	R = O	

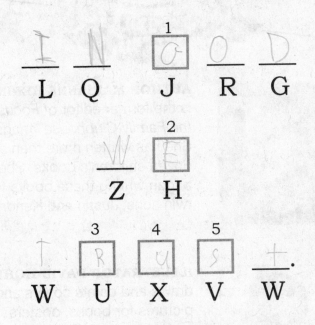

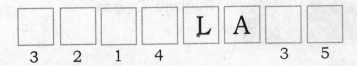

Go to *TheImaginationStation.com*
Find the cover of this book. Click on
"Secret Word." Type in the correct answer,
and you'll receive a prize.

135

AUTHOR MARIANNE HERING is the former editor of *Focus on the Family Clubhouse®* magazine. She has written more than a dozen children's books. She began writing these books for her twin sons, Justin and Kendrick.

ILLUSTRATOR DAVID HOHN draws and paints covers and pictures for books, posters, and projects of all kinds. He works from his studio in Portland, Oregon.

AUTHOR NANCY I. SANDERS is the bestselling and award-winning children's author of more than eighty books. She and her husband, Jeff, visited Lexington Green and toured the tavern. Find out more about her at *nancyisanders.com*.